CUPID & PSYCHE

BookSquirrel Publications

BookSquirrel Publication

Mahadev Totala Nager, Indore (M.P),452001
Regd Under MSME
Website:
www.booksquirrelpublication.com

"Cupid and Psyche"

By: Namraths Thukkaivel

ISBN: 978-93-89923-62-9

English and Hindi Anthology

Book Formatting: Aryan Verma

Cover Design: Ronak Chavda

<u>DISCLAIMER</u>

This Anthology is a work of fiction. The author has made sure that all the write-ups in this book are original, and without plagiarism. All the write-ups in the book are unique and belong solely to the Co-Authors. In case of any detection of plagiarism, neither the publication house nor the Compiler is to be held responsible.

The sole responsibility of the write-ups are on that writer.

<u>ACKNOWLEDGEMENTS</u>

I would like to thank my family for their untiring support and I would also like thank my professors (Sri G.V.G Visalakshi College for Women, Udumalpet, and Tamil Nadu) for their encouragement. Last but not the least I would extend my thanks to my Co-authors. Without them this would not have been possible.

Narmatha Thukkaivel
(Compiler)

Narmatha hails from Tamil Nadu. She is currently pursuing her Bachelor's degree in English Literature. She has a burning desire to write and speak. She is an orator who was selected to represent Tiruppur and Erode districts in the National Youth Parliament addressed by Honorable PM, Modiji. Writing is her passion. 'CUPID AND PSYCHE' is her third anthology as a compiler.

<u>MY DEAR CUPID</u>

Cupid and Psyche are mythological characters. The love between Psyche and Cupid ultimately unites them in a sacred marriage despite the obstacles. The daughter born to them was named as 'pleasure'. I was in the seventh heaven when I read this story. We have all heard the proverb, 'Art is long,Life is short'. In the same way, 'Love is long, life is short'.Love is immortal.The person you love becomes mortal being, one day but not the love. Everyone cannot be Savitri who conquered the death of her husband, Satyavan from fates over mastering power.

Weeks ago, our English mam told us as story tittle, "Why the sea is salt?" The story is about a pair of millstone which could produce anything for which their owner had taken a fancy. They could grind out silver,gold,diamonds as well as great quantities of love,gaiety,mirth,and peace. Our mam asked me what would, I grind if I were given to grind that millstone for one time.

I replied instantly that I would grind a better half for me, because materials never last long.Only true love lasts forever. My friend asked me, "Why don't you grind immense peace and gaiety?" I replied her, "With a good better half comes all the great values of life". My mam asked me, "Why don't you ask something for your parents?" I told her that I am here to take care of my parents. If my better half can give me everything,I can give everything to my parents .So, my decision remained the same that I would grind for my Cupid.

Our mam asked me what qualities should be possessed by the man who I grind for. I said that I need a man who would share not only my happiness but also my sadness and house hold works. He should have a good sense of humor. I don't want to dump all the works upon my better half. I want all the works to be shared. At that point, comes a complete equality of man and woman. I want a man who respect all women. I want him ask my opinions before taking serious decisions. He should be an optimist and friendly to everyone.He should be an honest and frank person without hiding anything from me.He should always be there to support and stand by me.

Of course, my better half too expects some qualities from me. If there comes a situation where I have to change my perspective on things in life for a good cause because of him, I would definitely accept his words.I would be very clear about choosing my betterhalf because he is the personI am going to share and spend my entire life. I think mutual trust and respect are the two important things essential for a happy married life

I here explained all the qualities that my future better half should possess. Last but not least,he should be loving and romantic too. Following is my promise to my better half.

"My dear love, I hope that we both make each other's bad days better. I will stand by you, till my last breath. No matter how many times we fight, I will never leave you at any cost. I will never stop loving you. I will keep my promise to you. Let our lives be a beautiful journey".

<u>A NONET ON LOVE</u>

Between Love and hallucination

He messes, seeing her in all

In the pond as a flower

In the vast sky as a moon

In the tree as bird

In soul as heart

What is this?

Oh sly

Love !!

<u>MY CLANDESTINE CRUSH:</u>

I caught the sight of more stars in the sky
Which made this guy, fly

That sparkle in her eyes
We're glittering like golden flies

That was her lip
Which made things around me flip

That was her hair
Which brought a sudden glare

That was her sight
Which made my heart and brain to fight

She became my clandestine crush
Which made me to rush

To see her everyday
Under the sky of gray.

Ishani Agarwal

Born and brought up in Kolkata, she has done her schooling and college from here itself. She is doing her Post Graduation at the moment. Ishani loves talking to people around, and is excited for this new beginning of hers. She has been a Compiler for 10+ Anthologies and in the process for more. She has also Co-authored 30+ Anthologies.Ishani is very happy with how her life is turning out now.

Insta handle: Ishani_agarwal_quotes

<u>THE FEELING OF LOVE</u>

Love is a unique feeling.

No matter where that person is,

No matter how he treats you,

But the moment you hear from them,

Your heart melts all over again.

That is Love,

But the problem is,

People take it very casually.

For, they know you are available for them all the time.

Therefore, they treat you like Garbage.

They do not care how you feel.

And when they want to get back, you still accept them. Why so?

Is it only you who loved?

Is it only you who cared?

If the answer is yes,

Then is the time and effort worth?

<u>What if</u>

What if I tell you?

That I am not perfect for you.

But still, I Love you.

What ifI tell you?

That I have flaws.

Scars that haunt me at night.

But still, I love you

What if I tell you?

I am an emotionally unstable person.

I get hurt often enough.

I cry in the dark.

I curl like a ball, and hide away if hurt.

But still, I love you.

Would you love me the same then?

<u>You promised, and you broke it</u>

You promised me that you would never leave me.

Yet you did.

You promised to hold my hand till my last breath.

Yet you left midway.

You promised to bring tears of joy.

Yet you always brought tears of hurt.

You promised your time and attention.

Yet, you never fulfilled them.

But still, even today, when you promise something,

I somehow tend to believe that you will fulfill this one at least.

<u>The sailor</u>

His touch felt magical.

It had been so many years to their marriage,

But even today,

Every time he returned from a voyage,

She would leap up in joy,

That night would always feel like a magic to her.

The way his touches would send tingles down her spine,

The way he would drink her with his eyes

Hungry and greedy.

The days he would visit, would go by in a daze.

And she would then always keep craving for those magical moments to return.

G. Deepika

She hails from Tamil Nadu. She is pursuing her Bachelor's degree in B.A. English Literature in Sri. G.V.G Visalakshi College for Women. This is her first anthology as a co-author. She hopes to reach many more heights in this field.

Life is a painting. I can draw a beautiful picture when you are beside me

I was an inexpensive stone once. You carved me into a beautiful statue now.

My dear darling,

You are my courage ;

You are my gaiety;

You are my belief;

You are my positivity;

You are my everything.

Love is a feeling. It travels in a lightning speed to make you smile.

Being loved by someone is a gift.

Sometimes love comes without a reason. But later it gives reason to Life.

Let you be the water; Let me be the leaf on it. Wherever you flow, I will be in that flow.

You made me a sculpture to keep on looking at my eyes.

Chirag L Sagar

He is a 1st year MBBS student studying at Srinivas Institute of Medical Sciences and Research Centre, Mangalore. He has been writing poems, articles and essays since the last 7 years. He has participated in various essay competitions conducted in and around the country. His best friend, Nihar, has always been his inspiration to do great in whatever he does. His dream is to become an Oncologist and a successful writer. Instagram : @chirag_cls18 Facebook : Chirag LSagar

<u>Just come over</u>

O 'sweetheart, I know we've parted ways,

But I still want you to know.

If you ever miss me, just come over.

If you think I'll ever forget you, then you're wrong.

 If you ever miss me, just come over, just come over"

I had no one except for you,

You had become more important to me than breathing.

I may not mean anything to you,

 But you mean everything to me.

 "Don't ever leave me" is what you always used to say

I have no more reasons to smile,

 As even you moved on like time.

 It had fallen for you, and still is,

My heart's crazy for you!

I did as you said,

 Only I know how I consoled my heart.

 Be happy wherever you are,

There was never anything between us anyway.

Doesn't matter how far away we are from each other's eyes,

We will meet everyday in the world of dreams.

This is as far as we were meant to be,

Now you must return.

If you ever miss me- just come over, just come over!

Dawn of Destiny

To live without you is like the heart without a beat,

 How shall we explain the true meaning of love to the world!

In this forbidden path of love,

 Let's do the impossible.

If we ever fall apart,

 We shall breathe no more.

 Oh Almighty,

 Tell us what's in store for us.

 We have,

We've only fallen in love.

 On the path of love, one encounters so many rivers.

 Even amidst a million storms, my heart somehow finds solace.

 There's so much strength in the heart's resolve.

It drives one from the waves to the shore.

Today the pictures have lost their colour and virtue;

The fate of lovebirds are being crushed,

In between others' hands after meeting.

The world has finally won it,

And love has lost to it.

Never have we thought,

That we'll separate after meeting.

Oh Almighty,

Tell us what's written in our destiny.

Falling in love is all we did,

And now we're separated apart, forever

A heart's anticipation

Again my heart realized,

It lets out a sigh anew.

I saw you once again,

Why did you go out of my sight the next moment?

I still wait for you,

Where is the peace in me without you?

My heart still yearns for you,

How do I explain this to you?

I still wait for you,

We both suffered the consequences of love.

We didn't lack faith in love for each other,

It was just the time, which wasn't by our side.

I still wait for you, I'll wait for you till the date you come back.....

Dr. S Geetha

Dr. S. Geetha is an Assistant professor of English who has 12 years of teaching experience. She has presented and published number of papers in national and international reputed journals. Her passion is teaching and reading books. She's guiding M Phil and PhD scholars. Her area of interest is ELT and Indian writing in English.

<u>ROMANTIC LIFE: AN AROMATIC LIFE</u>

Make us feel alive in all ways

Genuine romance exists in two-

Small acts of love and affection

They show they care each other

Romance is the key to keep

The sparks flying -without it

Relationships will soon

Loose its shine-For Love

So precious, so true

That mingles in all that I love.

Ahilabai V.

Ahilabai is an upcoming writer who has more interest in writing poems. This poem is a first try of her which acted as a milestone for her career. She is a great lover of literature.

<u>Dreams of togetherness</u>

Dreams of togetherness mold me alive

In the absence of your dreams I need departure from life

Dreaming is my supreme labor, that mold me alive

I love that because it serves as an embellishment for our life

I love that because it shows way for our desires

I need that as it serves me to feel you

I need that because it furnishes us with privacy

And dreams make me to reach our eternal world

I realize my completeness when I addicted to you

My dreams have power that will make us in unison.

Asfar Sithika.A

Ms. AsfarSithika.A is a lover of writing. She is the beloved daughter of Mr.M.ArifDheen and Mrs. A. Sofia Parveen. She is currently pursuing her B.com degree in Sri G.V.G. Visalakshi College for women, Udumalpet. She can express her thoughts by way of writing poems and quotes. She use to write poems in an inspirational way which have motivated and stimulated many. She loves and lives in music.

Instagram ID: achu_bts

Email:asfarachu@gmail.com

<u>CRAZY ON YOU......"</u>

The feel that never dies......

The hands that holds me tight......

The eyes that makes me cry......

The words that makes me fly......

The face that makes me happy......

The look that makes me die......

I want to make you 'my babe'......

I don't want to leave you away......

I just want to stay in your heart......

I don't want to move from you apart......

I just want to be your everything......

Even you don't see me as a thing......

I just want to make it right......

I just want to hold you tight......

You don't know how I feel for you......

You don't know how I think about you......

I don't want to make you sad......

I don't want to make you mad......

I am thinking of you over and over......

I don't know where I am supposed to hide......

It's a hard thing to forget you……

Even though I wanted to do……

Right now, I am feeling low……

I can't help me now……

My every pain is you……

And my only medicine is you……

<u>I will be your rose</u>

I will be your rose without a thorn…

Will you be the water that drops in my heart…?

When I look into your EYES…

I always melt down like ICE…

Even if it's raining out…

With you I feel so much hot…

Your eyes are my weakness

Stop undressing my soul with your eyes

It keeps on disturbing me

I couldn't sleep, couldn't eat

And I just think about you 24*7

I realized that love is not about chatting or meeting

It is all about thinking you every time.

M.Kavitha

M.Kavitha is an Assistant Professor of English who has more than 12 years of experience in teaching. She is currently pursuing her PhD degree from one of the reputed universities in Tamil Nadu. She has also presented and published papers in various UGC approved National and International Journals. She is a great lover of philosophy and likes to read and write books on it. She has acted as a resource person in various educational institutions and is currently guiding MPhil scholars. She is also a member in Board of Studies (BoS) which plays a vital role in syllabus framing.

<u>GUESS! WHO AM I?</u>

"LOVE"! The blow was loud enough when she wakes up from her dream. Priya's mind is filled with excitement thinking about the dream she had and feltbutterflies in her stomach. It's a kind of new experience which makes her feel like in heaven.

Dream....

Makes me inexhaustible

With pleasure and makes me

Unwrap to reveal myself

What happened!

Priya is an optimistic person with good looking features who just completed her college. She is a unique figure who never has desire for dress and ornaments. She lives happily in her own way. She loves to read books and spends most of her time in reading.

Her father is a Bank Manager who gets transferred every five years. This has made her travel so many places in and around the country.

Priya is a very friendly girl who looks beautiful and gets into the notice of anyone who meets her for the first time. As a result she had so many Friends of both gender. But she hates the word "LOVE", because to her, LOVE is worthless.

During their transfer at one point of time, they resided in a rental apartment. At that time, they became friendly with their neighbor-hood family. It is the first meeting of Ram and Priya. Ram is a very handsome, fair and intelligent boy pursuing his final year college. Priya joined the same college where Ram studied. He too is a unique person who like reading books and hated

"LOVE". They both had the same kind of likeness towards favorite things which made them to as intimate friends.

Even the members of both families became very close friends. Ram after completing his UG degree started to continue his PG in the same college. During his final year he attended the campus interview and got placed in a good reputed company which acted as a first and foremost reason for their separation. This is the first physical separation between Priya and Ram which

Also made themrealize their intense relation. Before leaving, he

presented her a book as a

Token of his remembrance.

Ram flies to America for his job and here comes a turning point. So far not realizing any kind of emotions or feelings for LOVE in her life, suddenly there happens a change. Missing Ram, and to fulfill his absence, she started spending most of her time only in reading the book presented by him. Because to her it seems to be something special and each time when she reads the book, she felt a new kind of feeling from it. This started to continue throughout her final year but without affecting her studies. She was perplexed of not knowing what to do.

Oh! What happened to me today?

I wish you were with me

To share everything I wanted to…

Since she spends most of her time with books, no one had a suspicion about her. Wherever she goes, she carries the book with her presented by Ram.

At one point of time she started to get dreams daily without any reason. She was often disturbed by this. From this time onwards, whenever she takes a book in her hand there comes a voice of echo saying

"GUESS! WHO AM I?

Trying to avoid my presence

But you escape me not…

Trying to convey this to Ram, but couldn't do so. She was astonished by this. Not knowing whom to say and what to do with it, she was so much disturbed. Priya was much worried thinking about Ram because there is no kind of communication from Ram after he left to

America. But she knows that he too likes her and loves her. To confirm this she wants to meet him and so she plans for it.

After completing her under graduation, Priya plans to do her higher studies in a foreign country, particularly in America hoping to reunite her meeting with Ram and to strengthen their relationship. She completed all the process and fled to America without informing this to Ram because she wants to give him a surprise. There she met with a failure

I came out with trust

But you made me longing

How come can you put me in a

Terrible condition!

She tried to find him, but she couldn't do so. She then realized

Being in LOVE…

What a wonderful thing!

Degree of mutual understanding

And true understanding

Of each other…

Your wisdom and silence

Though seldom to me

Like your presence when you are

Not nearby me…

I cannot comprehend

I think for I am actually

In love with my best friend.

The LOVE I have for you

Isn't the same I had yesterday?

But my LOVE has gotten stronger

The day will come to say

Just I LOVE YOU…

Having so much of dream about LOVE and LIFE with Ram, Priya awaits to meet Ram. But it was an utter failure. Priya happens to meet Ram's friend during her hunt for him and was shocked to hear the news from him. When she enquired to him about Ram, he said that he died in the airplane crash when he came to join for the job. More shocking to hear this and not knowingwhat to do, Priya burst out in tears.She ran immediately into the room to take the book presented by Ram. From the book again shehears the voice saying

"GUESS! WHO AM I?

Know not me

I am RAM…

Only now she realized the voice belongs to none other than Ram. Ram who was in deep love with her started to communicate to her through his soul. Their love is really intimate and their communication too became intense with love through the book. Priya after her completion of

Studies returns to her native and lived her life in the memories of Ram. Knowing that Ram is living with her through the book presented by him, she kept it very safely as a treasure and a precious gift. She laminated that book and started to share her love, emotions and feelings to Ram though the same. The book became her soul and companion as a living person "RAM" and she started to live with it. To her she lived with that book as her husband hoping that

The day will come for everyone

The very last act to perform

And I feel happy

Awaiting

For one such moment

To join with you and

And to say hold my hands...

"Falling" in LOVE is very often accidental without any effort or intention and it comes to be true only in the life of few people. One such love is the love of Priya and Ram who showed their intimacy through the book they like and proved to be the best ever loving couple.

It's my promise to love you

And will do it even after I die

Joining with you in heaven…

Jagannath Maharana

Jagannath Maharana was born on 30th September 2002 at Cuttuck. His current living place is Puri. He is a young writer and started his journey of writing since his school age. His writings are based on what he learns from his life. His first English poem is 'The necklace of Spider'. He has also written some Hindipoems like 'kuch tum ho to kuch hum ', 'badlahua Bharat ', ' Sabra ' etc

THE VALENTINE ROSE.

In the dawn, you shall bloom,

With some red petals,

To cover your head.

Some may pluck them,

On their honeymoon night.

The night of love,

To cover their bed.

Some may pluck them,

On their breakup day.

The day of heart break,

To cut their vein.

But, some may pluck them,

To decorate something

Or some may do,

To design their hair.

You shall become one day,

A bouquet of gladness.

That whoever keeps,

Gains the life of love.

I wish for sure,

To hold that bouquet.

And give it,

To my love on the rose day.

Dear Rose!

You are the love

Of the both loves,

Who always love you?

And from their life,

They shall never make you apart.

Dear Rose!

You are a love garland,

Like a necklace of red gold

Dear Rose!

You, by yourself,

Make two loves

To contemplate,

You make them

Ride and flow,

Dear Rose!

The loves you make,

Are always parallel

For this parallel world.

But, their distance

In between,

Always creates a care.

To move on forever

With that care,

I think of you

Oh! Dear Rose.

The care for you, with me,

Always goes.

Please, do me a favor.

Nothing, but a care.

Just grow and bloom

And give me a love dose.

Dear Rose!

What about love?

Is it a game?

Or a gain of fame?

Dear Rose!

You, the flower

Of Love God,

And the love,

Is incomplete

Without you.

For True love

Is a feeling?

Both hearts can hear,

Without any sign

And without any wine.

But nor can hear

Without you.

Of course,

The duration,

In between

You and your sign,

Is what we call?

'I Love you'.

And the time,

After your sign

That results,

For the wine,

Is what we call?

'I hate you'

But, in this present scenario,

Truth is that,the duration

Between both of them,

Is what we call'Avalentine love'.

Rutuja Kamale

Those motivated words reflects the toughest times. The inspiration in her eyes reflects those big dreams. With her perfectly heart melting words, she dreams to inspire all. Her aim is to become a motivational speaker. She believes that words have great power in them that can change a life. Motivating someone and help them achieve their dreams is what she dreams to be.

I found the one

I found the one my soul was always in need of

I found the one who makes me complete

I found the one who makes me laugh like an idiot by his crazy

Yet cute stuff

I found the one who stays silent and listens to

My things for hours without getting bored

I found the one my soul feels safe to be with

He's the one who cheers me up when I feel so down

He's the one who handles all my mood swings

He's the one who melts my heart with just a smile

He's the one who brings me my favorite chocolate, icecreams and

food

I found the one who's shy to express his love

But shows it all in the little things he does for me

I found the one who could turn the world upside down just to see me

smile

 I found the one whom I can trust blindly

I found the one my soul feels happy to make efforts for

I found the one whom I'd love to make smile

I found the one with whom I'd love to spend all my day off

I found the one I'd love to share my chocolates with

I found the one with whom I can do the craziest stuff together

I found the one who is as weird as me

I found the one with whom I fall in love every day a little more than yesterday

I'm in love with all the little things of him I'm totally in love with him

I found the one

My soul feels extremely happy to have

I found the one I feel proud to have

I found the one I'd love to share the rest of my life with

Being in love with him I found myself.

<u>Different from the rest</u>

She knew he was a bit twisted. Tough in behavior but soft with heart. The one with such a beautiful soul and with the prettiest smile. The one who cared for her so genuinely that made her fall in love with him so deeply.

He knew she was a mystery. The more he spent time with her, the deep he fell in love with her. Her understanding, her care, her affection, the way she cares for his smile, was something that made her different & special from the rest

<u>Deeply in love</u>

He never knew how deeply she loved him.

By helping him deal with his problems & making him smile, she proved it to him.

She never knew how deeply he loved her.

By taking responsibility of her smile, he proved it to her.

<u>Eye contact</u>

He never made an eye contact with her "You never pay attention" She complained.With a cute smile he replied "IfI keep staring at you, no doubt I will fall in love with you" And that's how a beautiful love story started.

<u>Maybe</u>

Maybe you were the reason for my smile

Maybe you were the reason for a while

I smiled like a shy.

Maybe it was you

Who left me cry.

Maybe you are the reason

I learned to be strong in my life.

Maybe it is the way you talk

Maybe it is your smile

That makes me go crazy.

Maybe it's your words

That makes me fall.

Maybe it's the deepest love I can ever fall

Maybe it's the way you ride straight into my heart & stole it.

Maybe you are the reason

I again started to live for.

Ayesha Shaikh

Ayesha Shaikh was born and brought up in Pakistan. From her childhood to her youth, she had always been an ambitious person, an outstanding student and a humble human being who has contributed to various occasions, activities, meetings, and collaborations for the benefit of the society. She says, "Writing is an art of composing your feelings within a text, and writing is not just a hobby but a passion, it's like describingcreatively about what a person is feeling. It's a magic".

<u>A Note to My Future Husband:</u>

I hope life has been treating you kind. I have no idea how I'd meet you. I have no idea if you even exist out there. Somedays, I wonder if you are really out there. The one who is the other half of me. The one who is just like me. Even in pain, my lips smile, when I remember the moments that have long gone. Despite going through such a tremendous heartbreak, I still have faith in love. I still have faith in you. Playing with my guitar at 2 AM in the morning on the terrace of my house, wondering if happiness is written in my fate too. This too shall pass they say, but some nights are too heavy, loneliness engulfs my soul as I lay there just staring at the ceiling above me with an aching heart and a desperate need to cry but I couldn't because all my tears have been dried. Each prayer that I make lifting my hands up to the direction of the sky, I ask for happiness to find its way to you and hug all of your sorrows away, leaving you feeling nothing but content. It is calming to know that you are out there someone who will love me on the days I am not so lovable. On the days, I am anxious or nervous. On the days, happiness no longer resides in me. On the days, I have no more stories to tell. On those days, I hope you stay. Sometimes, when the future seems bleak, it is better to hope. I hope you hold my hand to take a walk in the city on the days it rains profoundly. I hope you find happiness and beauty in the little things around you, just like I do. I hope you prefer to listen to songs with deep and meaningful lyrics instead of songs with beats that don't make any sense. I hope we melt into each other every morning as we wake up and every morning before going to sleep. I hope we write poems on each other's eyes and how they send us in a moment of ecstasy. I hope we never stop bringing out the best in each other. But most of all, I hope we never get tired of each other. I hope we never fall out of love. Until our paths cross, until we meet again. Love Always, your future wife.

<u>Tell him:</u>

Unspoken words inside me are many

Hidden feelings of my heart are plenty

The entire universe, he held it in the palm of his hands,

And as our fingers would collide

I experienced a feeling much divine,

In simpler words it cannot be described

In the walls of my heart his name I would inscribe

Lost at the words of his beauty, I gazed intently at his eyes,

The ones as dark and mysterious as the night sky

Losing him, forgetting him, or letting him go, I'd never try

My feelings are real that I wouldn't deny,

I never knew love could take someone so high,

I never knew by his side, I could forget the highs and lows of life,

Promising him with a letter still unsent to be his wifealone in the corner of my room, I cried

Finding someone that felt like him, I triedsomeone that felt like home, I tried finding far and wide

And if he was alive, I'd still choose him a million times over,

Just as the stars that are scattered in the sky, into a billion pieces,

My heart broke that way too,

Just as the vast universe, the human heart holds secrets too,

Wishing I would've confessed him sooner, I write this with an aching heart

The stars in the galaxy far away are the lamps of heavens decorating the grave of my beloved

A boy as beautiful as the moon,

A love lost too soon.

I'd be waiting for him in mid-June, on a Monday afternoon,

We'd talk all about our lives with each other till noon,

When I start to miss him more, I hope he returns too in monsoon,

So I can tell him, I loved you too

Happy moments without him are few, on my forearms I still have his name's tattoo,

This war of life and death, we will one day get through,

So that I can remind him, the best moments of my life are the ones spent with you,

No matter how far away we grew, I loved you too..

I loved you too….

Yazhini Ramamoorthi

Yazhini Ramamoorthi is an imaginative writer with more fantasy in her writings. Yazhini is a student of English literature at Sri GVG Visalakshi College for Women,Udumalpet and author of the new work titled "Which is our first conversation?"

<u>Which is our first conversation?</u>

I forget the day – when

I first saw your eyes,

I forgot everything in this world,

I starred at your attractive eyes,

Which deserves more love for me……

And what an excitement was that

Your eyes also did the same

Yeah we gathered to talk-but

Our eyes seemed to start talking with each other- soon

Our hearts also did the same,

My heart-beat fast,where

You found it, though I tried to hide

As a result,brain stopped its work

Hell – what an amazing day that was!

How can I express it to others?

My words just stuck in my vocals,

Again I try to hide it but

My smile shows everything…..

Our day ended with lots of memories,

And we found our destiny in that day

Yes, my life and my future is only you

I own you and most important your beautiful eyes!

R.Karthika

She is an enthusiastic girl who loves cricket. Her passion has begun just now which is writing. She is pursuing her Bachelor's degree in English Literature.

<u>To my love</u>

My love, you are the 8th wonder of the world. My days never end up without thinking you. You are the special one in my life. I still remember the day when I met you. I was totally tongue tied when I tried to talk to you .So I expressed all my feelings in this letter. You are in my soul at any each and every nook like my warm blood. I want to be your chocolate bite so that I can touch the succulent lips…You are like a sunshine in my life. You are the only reason for me to lead my future happily. The 26 alphabets are not enough for me to describe my love towards you. If you are the news, I will be the news reader. Stars make the dark night bright similarly you made my dark world bright. I don't want to miss you, my love. Now my life is in your hand accept and make my life glow like sunshine. Love you forever…

<u>THE CRY OF A SOUL</u>

It was a beautiful grove

In which he made his rove

When I was awoken

Everything was broken

You may flew into rage

Like a lion in the cage

But I will conquer you

Under the sky of blue.

You may go away

But I will not go astray.

My soul! You may forget me

But I dabbled you in my heart in glee.

Gowarthini.B

Gowarthini is an emerging writer from Tamilnadu .This is the first poem which helps her build a strong poetic career.

<u>ONE AND ONLY YOU</u>

You just entered in my life like a colored blossom

You just showed me the glow of my life

You just showed me the true love and care

You brought new changes in me

You showed me a new world with full of dreams and desires

You just held my hands and said 'I am there for you'

You made me feel your love inside me

You made me brave and bold

You made me a stronger person to face all the problems

Slowly, I am becoming you

Thiruvikram.S

He is Thiruvikram S from Tamil Nadu, pursuing DECE final year at KSRIT. He has been writing quotes and poems from his school days. He was inspired by Swami Vivekananda. He loves to write and express what he feels. He has been a co-author in various anthologies.

<u>LOVE</u>

The love is lovely to share andgreat to receive too.

Find the love where it is locatedwithin you to spread it with whole heartedly

Exchanging love is more powerful than the stuffs that we're doingwith more hope.

It is more beautiful, never treats anyone bad.

We all expect to receive tons of love from others

But we should also give that to others

Never hide it.

<u>The lord:</u>

Love is god. Ifyouwish to prevent it,God could writea rule that he can't even break.

Love holds the world:

Love is equal to the world. The love runs this world and ruins the other side by its shortage. It is important as thehumans need this world.

Angry lives in the love;

Angry lives within the love: "love and angry are the equal distant ones, never change their states".

The lovely nightmare:

Now a days all my dreams are filled with your memories, you have started to rule me even there!

Prachetan Potadar

PrachetanPotadar is one of the talented names in advertising industry when it comes to copy writing and creative direction. He became popular on social media by his hashtag #PenPaperPrachetan. Apart from work, Prachetan is hobbyist footballer. He has also contributed for "Save a Girl Child ".Mission. In short Prachetanloves to make positive impact on people around or with him.

<u>Forever</u>

SHE grabbed HIS hand with a blissful touch

They were sustained when situations were "too much"

Some peoplearound them was married or engaged

He uploaded just one word for her

"Forever"

HE was there for HER

When everything was in vain.

They shared a glass of everything

"Filled with fear, cheer and pain"

She clicked his picture as lifetime "Screen Saver"

With a perfect caption"Forever"

When they decided to tie their knot,

HE graced HER life

No matter what

She asked Him"will you please do me a favor?

"Let's update our status to

"Forever"

Forever & Ever

<u>Togetherness</u>

Open your eyes

I am here with light

We evaded dark Past

In the middle of the night

Up with your eyes

Stop worrying about your darkness

Your heart has light

Which showed path of "togetherness".

<u>One More for Him & Her</u>

One more time

One more TEAR

They are back together

Without any FEAR.

With Firm "Faith"

No more "Hate"

They won "The Bet "

When they met

Cast was ACTIVE

Religion was 'RACE'd

Both were pissed off

When everything was "MESS"ed.

Their bond cleared all myths

They are back now

With dear and tear

<u>Happily Ever After</u>

She was an "Attitude"

When I was "Glory"

She ruled my life

As a Moral of the "Story"

It is all set to keep

The Magic Alive

This is beautiful fairy-tale

About "How we survive?"

I am going to be part of

Your" love and Laughter"

Title of the our love story is

"Happily Ever After"

Uma V R Parvathy

Uma V R Parvathy is an upcoming poet and writer who predominantly write on themes such as 'the supernatural', 'the human mind and soul' and 'love beyond life'. She currently lives in Thiruvananthapuram, where she was born. She did her master's degree in Business Administration and wrote business newsletters for organization. Her poems have been published in several online platforms and books, some of which have been rewarded. She is a vegan, a polyglot and is looking forward to publishing her first work of fiction "Evangeline". Her book containing forty-eight one-liners and quotes is titled "Born with the Fire", where she explores various contradictions, has already been published.

<u>ARTHUR - I LOVE YOU!</u>

Arthur - I love you.

Oh, Lord of Warriors, where are thou?

My birth: to be thy slave.

Nights fell, days rose - my world ends.

The moon; her lovers teased - the wolves.

Thou are my moon!

In the skies I long to see thee.

Just a wolf, I become!

Yonder thy several lovers my Lord!

That night thou loved me.

Thou strength, my charm - both united.

The wait of a hundred births.

My tears, madness, pain - all for thee:

I thy only wolf; my sword pierces thy heart!

The sweetness of my breasts and thy blood!

In the skies I see thou everyday.

Thou the warrior; I the queen beyond the seven destinies!

Arthur - I love you! I killed you!

Shobika Balaraman

ShobikaBalaraman is an aspiring bard and writer. She, an endearing daughter is ardent in writing treatises and to a surprise note, her gaze turned on into short story writing. It is this, her first short story in the theme of love. She hails from Udumalpet, an alluring town from where she is pursuing her UG 3rd year in English Literature at Sri GVG Visalakshi College for Women.

<u>The Cupid's Day!</u>

"The morrow was so bright

The heart so to reach the height."

The summer morning was so bright than ever that it indirectly disclosed her something parted was waiting ahead to reunite. It was that day she wanted to cherish in her lifetime. Also, it was the day that she wanted to reload and live again. In an interim, it was the day that caused her to believe in magic. "Was it the plan of God? Or was it the play of Cupid? wondered the girl.

May 12, 2016

"Lia! Liaa! Liaaa!", screamed her mother from the kitchen to wake her up early at least that day. "It was 8a.m. and she is still in bed", mumbled her mother and went inside the bedroom. She again tried to wake her up and ended up in anger for her daughter sleeping without any fear of the day for her HSC result. Lia's mother without any contemplation took the glass of water from the wooden shelf placed near Lia's cot and sprinkled some water from the glass on Lia's covered face with "Lady Boss" imprinted royal blue colored bed sheet. With a sudden scream, rose the dawn of the family "Lia". Lia was traumatized by her mother's act because she knew her mom, who had never done this before to wake her up since she only throws any silver plates and vessels as much as that would least hurt but wake her up. Quietly realizing the fact, Lia woke up from the bed and arranged her pillows and bed sheets in order. Her mom was staring at her actions and uttered a sentence that gave Lia a chance to chill her mom in reply. Mom said, "Maybe you can repay your sleeping time after becoming an IAS officer." Lia replied, "Only if you wake me with those steel vessels." They both laughed for a moment and stepped out of the cherry reddened room with classy lights that even sparkle in days. Lia took bath and dolled up with a classy vesture that would surely stun her own eyes that it always gives her a confidence to beat the battles that about to play. Lia's father was waiting in the living room to take her to check the result and get her admitted in "Loyola College", the best of all colleges in the state. They both left for her school to check the result. When they both sat in the school waiting bench, she gazed so furious that even the passer-by chilled her with soothing words to worry not since she will score great. It was 8.59 a.m. and Lia's body became too cold. At sharply 9 a.m., the result sheet was stuck in the school main board and everyone reached the board like hungry lion chasing to hunt for its prey except Lia. Lia's dad was so cool that he actually knew his daughter will score good enough whereas he didn't expect any state or district ranks. Lia after moments reached the board and tried to look for her name in the board."There it is!" heard a voice behind her and surprisingly not it wasDhara, her friend since KG. Lia looked into the name and was quite a bid stunned by her high score. Then with the same shock, she went near her dad and confessed her score as 89 percent. He was ecstatic to know his daughter's high score and had a relieved sigh to get her admitted in Loyola College. He was also glad, to paint in black the people who discouraged Lia. After completing certain process in the school, they both left for Nungambakkam from Sowcarpet. They were stuck in traffic for few minutes since the whole city was filled with people of other places running for college admissions. They finally reached Sterling road in Nungambakkam where Loyola College was located. Lia's father dropped her near the large gate of the college entrance and left for home since he wanted his dearest daughter to learn things and go on in her own as her college admission be the first attempt. Lia went inside the college campus after waving a goodbye to her dad. She queried where the admission hall was and as per the directions by a fellow mate who just came from the admission hall, she reached it though. It was where the entire bunch of good books hailed to get admit in one of the topmost colleges of arts and science in India. When Lia was making out her way to settle, there heard someone calling out her name, "Liaa! Liaaa!" Lia turned back noticing a girl with doe-brown eyes winking at her like already known. She was short, quiet a bid stout like her neighbour Sheela aunty and her face was pale pink with countable acne and black spots. At first, Lia couldn't recognize her and then she could make it up that she was her

Coimbatore home's neighbour, Shreya. Lia was at last happy to see a known face there, who could accompany her the rest of the process. Since it was Lia's first attempt in getting through stuffs alone, she expected to be with someone who could just accompany her. After having the usual conversation like, "How are you, where do you live now, why you left the place" and so on.., they both settled in a stone bench under the large tree with mellow leaves shining along the sun. When Shreya asked for water, Lia took her Blue glass bottle imprinted the same, "Lady Boss" as her bed sheet out from the royal blue colored bag and gave her. At that matter of moment, a sweet voice was calling out Shreya's name behind them. Lia turned back suddenly as she sensed the voice was from someone she knew before. To a surprise note, it was Arjun, Shreya's elder brother. Lia was stunned seeing him as he was quite special from her childhood. He seemed so tall, fit as a film hero whereas his wide eyes, hawk nose and round face suited his perfect Indian fair complexion. He was as astonished as Lia. He came near her and with his face turned pink, his eyes met hers. Shreya seeing her brother thought he was unaware of who Lia was and told him "Hey June! Don't you remember her? She is Dev uncle's daughter, Lia." He playing the track right replied, "Oh! Yeah. That little daddy's girl, right? How grown up her is nah? Shray!" Lia smiled at his cute attempt and retained silent for few minutes until the "who and why" game got over. Shreya introduced her handsome brother to Lia and asked whether she remembered those childhood days playing together where Arjun protecting them from other fellow street mates for their mischievous behavior. Lia, her face turned pinker than Arjun's replied for Shreya's questions then. They three sat in the stone bench waiting for the girls' name being called for the admission process. It was only Shreya talking in loads whereas Lia and Arjun spoke a bid in response. Shreya's name was popped out in the display screen and she went to the admission hall leaving them both together. After Shreya left, a few minutes later, Arjun gained his breath and turned towards Lia to converse with her. He began like, "Ah.. Hey Lia! How are your parents? It's been years to see you finally and I can't even imagine you grew up too quick like Shray and now here to hit your UG degree. "Whereas she replied, "Mm. They are great. By the way, time runs like it pause not for even a moment, right? In an interim, you too grew up so damn quick whereas I can't even relate your present face to your old beings." The conversation went on where they both became quite comfortable and began to get to know each other's past life happenings after their separation. After half an hour, Shreya arrived and saw them chit chatting noticing not even her there, where it was quite bizarre for Shreya seeing her brother conversing with a happy face to a girl. Since, Arjun wasn't a person who converse with girls for more than 2 minutes, Shreya could sense that something was fishy in him after meeting Lia. Soon displayed Lia's name on the board. Lia went to the admission hall then, leaving the siblings there in the stone bench. Shreya then noticed Arjun blushing for something and confirmed that the poor soul was attacked by the Cupid. Shreya with no relatable questions of his blush, discussed about her admission process in purpose to not let her head in the game of Cupid. She was actually quite happy for them both getting into the cupid's leela since, she had a beautiful bond with Lia. After half an hour, Lia arrived and narrated her weird behavior inside the Admission hall. They left the college campus then. They three went for lunch outside the campus after informing their parents about the succession of admission process. They had a great feast in the nearby DindigulThalappakatti restaurant and also memorable conversations which brought back them to their childhood days. They three went to some more places nearby to indulge in fun a bit more. It was a magical day for them since after years the persons who never thought to meet in their wildest dreams met so. The entire day was fun filled for Shreya whereas it was quite more than great for Arjun and Lia to get to know them in person in loads. Lia's father called her to know where she was and told her to bring Shreya and Arjun home. Lia told that they were at Express Avenue and soon she'll be reaching home along with them both. After reaching home, Arjun and Shreya were given a great dinner. After the dinner, Lia and Shreya went to the terrace to chill themselves. Fifteen minutes later, Arjun joined the fun club. They three were as blithe as they were during their childhood days. They played truth or dare game then, to know even more stuffs of each in person. In between, Shreya got a call from her mom. When she narrated the happenings of the day and their stay then at Lia's home, Shreya's mom was as glad as them and told her to give the phone to Lia's mom to converse with her long-awaited family friend. Shreya went down to reunite their long-awaited family friends. At that matter of time, Lia asked Arjun why he had left her home without even a Goodbye greet during them shifting the home from Coimbatore. He replied that, since being a reserved person, he couldn't express his emotions and feelings of letting his special person part from him leaving for somewhere far. Also, it was hard for him to see her part him with no contactable source possible then. So, he left her home that day without letting her know how horrified he was and added up that, "This time I suppose the Cupid is high since he made me to even stare your tenebrous eyes and funny nose like every damn day from July 1st week."Lia couldn't get the sense and asked what he actually meant by saying "every damn day from July 1st week." Arjun with a blush on his pink and light red combo colored cheek replied, "I mean from July 1st, I'm officially your college senior, Ms. Dahlia Dev." After hearing the words of Arjun, Lia turned speechless. Moments later, trying to turn normal, Lia held her breath and letting out replied him without a pause, "Whattttt? Are you serious? You mean, you are pursuing your UG now at Loyola. Gosh, I didn't expect such a twist from cupid coz I thought this time he'll at least not part us whereas we can meet when you visit Shreya. But really man, who knows what god planned for us""Relax kiddo", replied Arjun. "Oh man, I'm trying to. But, anyway, your junior is waiting for the Cupid's game from July 1st week and so get ready for the battle my dearest senior", said Lia. Arjun blushed in response whereas silence filled then. The breezy wind made them travel ticketless that night and soon Shreya called them both down to rest. The whole family slept in peace that night whereas the Cupid's prey was indulged in alluring memories of that day and upcoming happenings then.It was a perfect cupid's day, the allured soul wondered.

"The swain in search of a leman,

So, the cupid's day was to help that human".

K.Balaa Thiribura Sundari

She is BalaaThiriburaSundari who hails from Tamil Nadu. She loves writing and loves to express her thoughts,through it. She wants to become a good writer and she says that one day she will achieve it and make her parents proud. She believes God and with him on her side everything is possible for her.

<u>To the one who broke my heart</u>,

Each time whenever I visited your home. You are the antagonist whom I thought to avoid .Still remembering the ridiculous days where I walked pride. Not as egoistic,but to show you that I won't care for you .Years rolled,and something deep I felt inside. Where the face of one I hate pictured in front .I Thought it as a nightmare and tried to forget. But it started to fill in my heart. Once heard some words said by someone, that hatred automatically gets changed into love. I thought it as a false statement. But Cupid made it factual by, pointing arrows towards me, where you became protagonist in my life. Everyone felt my love except you. Fancied myself that he was loving too. Sneakily watched his picture in mobile with lots of trouble. I got a chance to talk with him first, waiting for him to reply my text. That day shivered me like being in freezing point. Finally we became good buddies. Waited with hope for him to express my love. My doubt cleared, he loved but not me. My heart broken and shredded tears when he confessed his love for another girl. He felt grief for her and I felt grief for him. I realized even a boy truly loves a girl. I mocked at him to cease his blubbering. But no one to wipe the anguish within me. Deep inside felt lost in a unknown world. Dreamt that you will be my stress buster. Where my pillow made that job in wiping tears. I felt that I was unlucky to have his love.

And I realized, he was failed to have my love. I wish God to keep my love unknown to him. Still now I love him in my dream, he was totally different in my dream. There he loved me in turn. He cared me Like the morning ray along with its bliss, like the night along with its darkness, like the rain along with its breeze, like the flower along with its fragrance, like the ocean along with its gurgling sound, like the sky along with its cloud, like the shell along with its pearl, like the body along with its soul. You had been there in my dreams. once I thought to end my life, then I thought if I ended my life I can't see you in my dream who loved me more than anything. One day you will definitely come to know about my love for you, that day you feel the anguish like hell in your heart. That time you will search for me, everywhere. I will not be there in this Inn but I promise you, that I will be there with you deep in your heart.

Dwelling inside you
The tired soul gave up with everything
 Once it was not tired over anything
 Because of attraction towards a soul
 Fell in love which ended in fowl
 Got more scares deep in heart
Those torment enlarged daily to peak
 One day the soul got detached
The soul in the air got ached

It became the oxygen you breathe

When you inhaled I went inside you

 And into the heart where I felt you!

Will be inside you until the beat gets halt.

<u>Born to hold yours hand</u>

In the life of sea, you are my shore

Where happiness is hidden like Earth's core

Safest locker in this world is your hug

Where I feel like being inside a shrug

Melodious tune I ever heard is your heart beat

That encourages me every time to feat

My stress buster is your shoulder

Where I'm going too tight you holder

My happiness is your presence

Don't fill me with anguish by your absence

I can't forget that dream last night

Everything happened in my life right

Unfortunately these became my dream

By making me weeping and to scream

Now I wish these things to happen in real

Praying not to play with me in cruel

And I wish the Cupid to shoot the arrow at you

As he pointed at me once towards you

Found you rambling inside the fence

Where flowers spreading its fragrance

The Meadows welcomed our love by dance

But waiting to hold your hand by chance

Felt like already bonded at previous birth

When my heart showered with endless mirth

Again found you beside me after a long gap

Still waiting for you to propose me like sap

Tired of waiting, for you to make my valentine

Finally decided to propose you and make mine.

S.Vinodini

Vinodini a 19 year old lass,halis from Udumalpet,Tamilnadu. She is pursuing her Bachelor's degree in English Literature. She is fond of cricket and music.She writes to bring the truth of life to the light.

<u>LOVE AND MARRIAGE</u>

Shivanya is a rich girl. Her parents bring whatever she wants. She studied well in her higher secondary and joined college at Meerut. Kumar is a handsome boy from a middle class family. His mother works as a domestic helper in many houses. He joined college at Meerut. Shivanya stayed in hostel and they both joined in the same course. Shivanya couldn't stay in hostel without seeing her parents. She started weeping in the class for many days. Kumar tried to console her and they became friends in the second Year. Shivanya was attracted by the affection and care of Kumar and fell in love with him. One day she proposed Kumar and he accepted her love. They went to park, beach, movie and restaurant. Now they cannot live without the other. In an interview Kumar got selected for a job in Australia. In the meantime Shivanya told her parents that she loves Kumar and wanted to marry him. Their parents opposed their love due to Kumar's middle class background. Kumar went to Australia and kept in touch with Shivanya. He talked to her for long hours. She was happy that he doesn't forget her love. After few days he stopped taking her calls and didn't reply her messages. This made her sad. Kumar couldn't connect with her through calls as he was in the situation where he was not supposed to make calls. But he believed that Shivanya would wait for him. Shivanya did the same. She waited for him. She remembered the lovely days spent with him. After a long gap, he returned to India. And he asked her father to marry her daughter. Her father got shocked and remained silent. Her father accepted the love because Kumar was then a well-to-do person and his character is also good. Her father decided to marry Shivanya to Kumar. The story ended in wedding bells. This is a simple story but I want to convey the younger generation a truth. Money is not the only solution for everything but a sufficient amount of money is essential to satisfy our basic needs. Kumar is an ideal youth. If he had thought, he could have eloped with Shivanya and later he can lead his life with the money of Shivanya's dad. But that will not bring self-respect to him. When he could stand by his own legs, he approached Shivanya's dad for marriage. And Shivanya's dad sees only the present situation of Kumar. He doesn't avoid Kumar as once he was a son of a domestic helper. The only thing he want is to see her daughter live a happy life and every dad wants the same. It is what gives meaning to life. But ending the love in marriage brings the true essence of life.

Dipang Ghosh

Dipang Ghosh, resides in Delhi NCR. He is a writer as well as an artist who loves to sketch. He is very obsessed with collecting coins and novels. He has been a co-author in many anthologies. Recently he got certificate from the India Book of Records for his contribution in a world record holder anthology. He is a science enthusiast as well. In future he wants to be an entrepreneur.

<u>Concept of love</u>

A feeling or an activity?

Something that motivates us or something that's just a series of events?

Something that our soul enjoys or something that's just a social show off?

Something that's felt or something that demands a feeling?

Something precious or something that demands your precious ones?

A wall to protect or a property to demand a right on?

Something that demands presence or something that demands time?

A story to tell or a mistake to hide?

A forever precious love for someone or a bad experience to refer to?

Someone for whom our simple "Hi" matters a lot or someone to whom your texts containing cheesy lines don't matter at all?

Someone who respects your choice or someone who forces you to choose?

When you come home tired, someone who can just sit with you and have lots of talks which soothe your soul or someone with whom you find excuses to escape?

Someone who is there for you during your worst and the best times or someone who is there during your best times?

Someone who helps you to gain many skills or someone who is just there to cheer you?

<u>You</u>

I don't think you will

Ever fully understand

How you've touched my life

And made me who I am.

I don't think you could ever know

Just how truly special you are,

That even on the darkest nights

You are my brightest star.

You've allowed me to experience

Something very hard to find,

Unconditional love that exists

In my body, soul, and mind.

I don't think you could ever feel

All the love I have to give,

And I'm sure you'll never realize

You've been my will to live.

You are an amazing person,

And without you I don't know where I'd be.

Having you in my life

Completes and fulfills every part of me.

Worship

My religion is you.

To worship every inch of you,

To worship every bit of you,

With praying hands and beseeching lips I worship you.

I worship every inch of your skin,

I worship every inch of your inner being creating our own heaven

Each other's hearts and minds

Filled with only love without anyadulteration...

You be my goddess and

I will be your devotee.

<u>Thanks for being there</u>

Thanks for the things you do for me...

Thanks for being the friend of that boy who never had the courage to talk with other girls.

Thanks for being the best friend and melting my ice frozen heart.

Thanks for accepting all of the good and bad things in me.

Thanks for always understanding my troubled mind and soothing it.

Thanks for keeping up with me through all the thick and thin, never letting me go.

Thanks for always listening to my chatter, blabber and what not.

Thanks for always being there for me.

Thanks for loving me like you do, really grateful for that.

Truptimani Kumbhar

He loves to reads novels and to express his feelings thorough his writings.

<u>ONE HUNDRED LOVE SONNETS</u>

I don't love you as if you were a rose of salt, topaz, or arrow of

carnations that propagate fire;

I love you as one loves certain obscure things, secretly, between the

shadow and the soul.

I love you as the plant that doesn't bloom but carries the light of

those flowers hidden within itself

And thanks to your love, the tight aroma that arose

From the Earth, lives dimly in my body.

I love you without knowing how or when, or from where,

I love you directly without problems or prides;

I love you like this because I don't know any other way to love,

Except in this form in which I am not, nor are you

Close your eyes, let them close with my dreams...

<u>THE LANGUAGE OF LOVE</u>

Your every untold word spoke of love

Your visuals spoke of love in silence

I felt each words purgated from your heart

I can feel your presence somewhere nearby

Far from somewhere it came

All the way around and reached me.

I know it spoke of love.

I know they were meant for me.

I could feel each word

Taught for one to understand

But they spoke of love and pain as well

I am very happy with that

You understand me so well

I am obliged you are a gem

I have known.

These qualities put you high in my thoughts

All I can tell is I adore you from my heart.

Love doesn't mean achieving what you want.

Love also means understanding the heart.

Love also means sacrificing the one you love.

Giving up is also a love.

Love has dimensional perspective.

It can be taken in any way you want.

Love has different colors

You can paint love in any colors you want

Actually, love neither has any shapes nor any colors

It's we who give shape and color

Nidhi Parmar

Nidhi Parmar, the writer of the poem delineating you, is currently pursuing BDS in Jamnagar. She fancies writing poetries, music and art. She is a thriving poetess who has taken part in two anthologies so far.

<u>**DELINEATING YOU:**</u>

This magma that erupts

Isn't it too sudden, too abrupt?

I feel them, butterflies, with just a thought of yours

Towards the glee, you open all my doors.

With you, nothing feels incorrect

Every moment, is just as you are, so perfect

With you beside me, I can walk a thousand miles

I could always go on with all your pretty smiles

I never knew the happy, until you came along;

You're my perfect lively song

I live in every moment I spend with you

Like I've found a world, a life so new.

A million times I would want you to

Call out my name, just the way you do

My days are no longer blue;

For my heart finds solace in you

You lit up my dark days;

You'll be my sunshine always.

Every gust of wind that touches my skin

Reminds me of your warmth so keen

The most unexpected miracle you are

That little shining light that shone from far

Soothing as a mother's lullaby

That let all my frets run by

I found you, a fine, beautiful mirage

That led all my agonies to the roads of sabotage

You're the finest ever art,

That'll always stick to the wall of my heart

No matter how much I try to hold you at bay;

It all comes back to you at the end of the day

Maybe you'll ever need me;

But I need you, so much more than you'll ever see

Along with every shooting star, I'll blow;

The wishes that ever would you say you won't let go.

Hemakg

Hematries to expose her darkest phase to light with a hope like a Sun which fell into the ocean evening but rises again with sharp rays.

<u>Three sayings of two people's one and only love</u>

You said

"I never had, I don't have and I'll never have feelings on me!"

I said

"I never had, I don't have and I'll never have thought of unloving you!"

God said

"I never had, I don't have and I'll never have revealed the end of your LOVE story!!!"

S.Shanmugavalli

S.Shanmugavalli belongs to Cuddalore. She has adopted writing as a hobby, and at present she has started her career as a writer. Her love, passion towards literature is seen in her writings. She strongly believes that writing is the way of expressing oneself through words.

<u>LOVE AT FIRST SIGHT</u>

Until I saw you

I never believed in

Love at first sight

You're the first man I love

And I don't know how

You were in my side

When everyone started to hide

You were in my happiness

And in my sadness

When you hold me my emotions are clear

And that made me to be with you here

I like to listen to your heartbeat as if it was my own

I would like to be in your love which you have shown

I like to start my day with you

Which the feelings and the words new

To describe that happiness

As it is a bond of endless

You made my life brighter and new

And that made me love you

You were in my thought throughout the day

That made me alive throughout the way

Your thoughts made me brighter in my dark filled room

That makes my heart filled with bloom.

<u>WORDS CAN ALSO EXPRESS LOVE</u>

With you I feel so fine

 And believe me love is not a crime

 With you I am everything

 And without you I am nothing

I love you more than words could say

With my heart full of gay

I think of you each night and day

 And for ourselves I used to pray

You are the Sunshine of my life

I wish us to be husband and wife

Please don't go away

As I promise our love will not fade away

LOVE IS PURE AND TRUE

My love for you is pure and true

I never stop thinking about you

I promise to be with you forever

When everyone crumbles never

You are my only one

Whom was made to won

And I feel happy and fine

When I realize, you are mine

My heart beats only for you

This feeling to me of you is new

Our love has to cross hardship

And that make a strong bond in our relationship

<u>LOVE</u>

Love is a feeling - feel it

Love is a blessing – get it

Love is a challenge – face it

Love is unconditional – give it

<u>LOVE- A GOOD COMPANY</u>

Love is of four

It doesn't bore

Love doesn't need money

Because it is a good company

Paramasivam

Paramasivam has been working at an MNC Company for the last 5years. He was an HR Executive. Writing love poems, reading books are always a wonderful feeling to him. He loves to read a lot. He wants everyone around him to stay positive and strong. He loves to travel a lot.

<u>A SOULFUL CONNECT</u>

Typing to push the rusted gears over the fossils of once unwinding love,

I learned how to walk past leaving behind those clogged bloody drains,

Where the time was not holding up its power to pass by

As it was difficult and suffocating, dingy and dark.

Hiding the vulnerable authentic within,

I tried my best to fire a rage,

That shall lit the path up,

Which I had decided to map,

By connecting the sliced threads between

My heart and soul, soul and heart.

Am I moving forward?

I don't know but yes,

I am moving to a place which is shoving away thedarkness

By explaining the secrets of true soul to connect,

By embracing the little inner voices and heartful

Rumbles decorated in the way of echoing warm breeze of the new dawn,

Where no one can ever lose or win.

Chandani Bhatia

Chandani Bhatia is a housewife / teacher by profession and writer by passion.She loves to write on whichever topic she gets .Her poems were published in a book 'Ishq Undivided'.

<u>Love–essence of romance</u>

They are sitting

On a bench

On that rainy day

Totally drenched

They had a talk

Which left

Them deep into

All themselves

He offered her

A warm tea cup

With the tinkling

Of raindrops to hear

She was offended

Seeing a single cup

Made him

To sip up

It wasa very

Unusual day

They were meeting

On a rainy day

They left each other

With formal goodbyes

But something was felt

Deep in their eyes

Hope to meet again

Made them happy

Was it all?

Cool or in a jiffy….?

NOWHERE! SOMEWHERE!

Life left us nowhere

But love made it everywhere

Wherever I go

I see love

Love everywhere

Love everywhere

Love in a flower

Love in a tower

Love in air

Love in fair

Just everywhere

Just everywhere

But today

Lost is the

True love

Just somewhere

Just somewhere

Lost in the darkness

Of ego and revenge

Causing us to

Curse love

Just somewhere

Just Nowhere….

Asutosh Behera

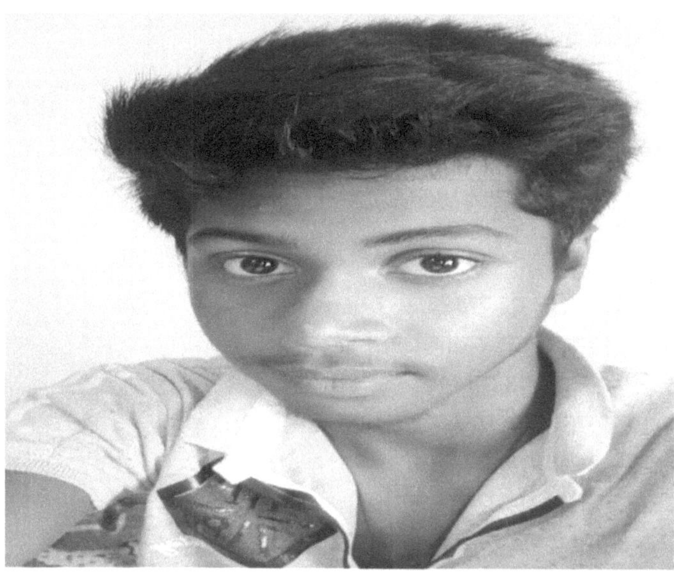

आशुतोष बेहेरा का जन्म २९ जनवरी २००४ में पूरी, ओडिशा में हुआ था। पढ़ाई के आयु में निकल पड़े हैं लिखने की सौगाता में। अधिकतर हिंदी भाषा का प्रयोग करते हैं लेकिन कभी मन थिरकता है तो अंग्रेजी और उड़िया का भी प्रयोग करते हैं। उनका पहला कविता "प्रेम की कश्ती में दुनिया" है। इस तरह के कुछ कविताएं कुछ किताबों में छापी जा चुकी है।

<u>आवारे की प्रेम गाथा!!</u>

आसमान में सुरीले हवाओं का शोर था।
दिल में कुछ था नहीं लेकिन,
किसी को ढूंढने वाला शोर था।
एक ही तो दिल था मेरा उसे लेकर आ गया।
लौटते समय देखा तो उसे भी कहीं रख के आ गया।
मेरा दिल उसके तील पर आ गया।
अरे यह क्या कर दिया मैंने,
मेरा दिल तो उसके तिल पर रख के आ गया।
(वहां से निकलते समय कुछ सवाल किया था मैंने।)
घर में एक पूजा है तुम आओगी ना?
दीपक के नीचे बैठकर तुम्हें परखने का मौका दोगी ना?
मैंने अपने वचन का स्वागत कर लिया,
अब तुम अपने बात को मुकम्मल करोगी ना?
उसने घर पर अपना पहला कदम रख लिया था।
और अपने वचन का पालन भी कर दिया था।
उस दिन मैं थोड़ा व्यस्त था।
फिर भी उस के लिए बेबस था।
मेरी आशा नहीं थी लेकिन वह आ चुकी थी।
जिस्म धरा पर थी लेकिन निगाहें आजाद घूम रही थी।
उसने मुझे देखा मैंने उसे देखा,
शायद निगाहों का विनिमय हो चुका था।
शायद मुझे देख उसके निगाहों की प्यास बुझ गई थी।
लेकिन अब भी मेरे होंठ कि रूह चीख रही थी।
कुछ दिन तक हमारा मिलना तो ठीक था।
लेकिन हमें क्या पता,
यहां कौन किस के मन का मालिक था।
फिर कुछ दिन बदले कुछ रात बदली,
कदाचित बदली उसकी चाहत भी।
दोनों आपस में बिनवाकिफ थे,
शायद बदल चुकी थी मेरी चाहत भी।

तेरे और मेरे ख्यालों को कभी ना कभी तो मिलना था।
हां मुझे तुमसे प्यार है यही राज़ तो खोलना था।
मेरा जिस्म धरा पर ठीक था।
शायद उसने कुछ कर दिया है,
मेरा रूह उसके प्रेम मैं लिन था।
हृदय का तापमान अधिक था।
उसकी निगाहें थोड़ी कमजोर।
उसके नाम मैं ही इसारा था।
बस उसके लफ्ज़ कहीं ओर।
फिर एक दिन आया।
मैंने थोड़ा साहस बटोर के लाया।
सोचा मजाक-मजाक मैं ही कह दूंगा।
अगर दिल ना भरे तो मजाक कह दूंगा।
इस मजाक को उसने इजहार कह दिया!
भोला भाला हूं मुझे चालाक कह दिया!
उसे महफिल से फर्क पढ़ता नहीं यह साफ कह दिया।
यह प्यार है शायद साफ यह मुझे कह दिया।
उस दिन से मुझे चांद सुहानी लगती है।
यह कहानी अब मुझे बेगानी लगती है।
यह सच्चाई मुझे दिल की लगती है।
जिस कहानी मैं बाधा ना हो,
वह आवारी लगती है।
वह बेगानी लगती है।

Anushka Bhati

AnushkaBhati is a 17 years old budding poet, and generally writes about love. This is her third anthology as a co-author. Instagram @suroor_e_shayari

<u>वो हमेशा यही कहता है</u>

हमारी मुलाकात होने पर वो चुप सा रहता है,

मैं उसे एक टक देखती हूँ तो आँखों से कुछ कहता है।

उसे खबर नहीं है, पर मुझे उसका यूँ बाते करना अच्छा लगता है।

मैं जब कुछ कहूँ तो बेशक वो सुनता है,

पर मेरी बातों से ज़्यादा वो आवाज़ से बहकता है।

तरी आवाज़ में बहुत सुकून है, वो हमेशा यही कहता है।

यकायक फिर वो मेरा हाथ थाम लेता है,

हर बार वो ये ही शरारत करता है।

मुझे मदहोश आंखों से वो कुछ यूँ तकता है,

मेरी आँखों में खोकर मेरे जज़्बात पढ़ता है।

कुछ इस तरह वो मेरी पलकें झुका दिया करता है।

तेरी आँखों से मुझे सुरूर चढ़ता है, वो हमेशा यही कहता है।

साहिल पर साथ बैठे होते है जब, तो हाथ कांधे पर मेरे रख देता है,

मासूमियत से फिर वो मेरे और पास सरक जाता है।

हवाएं मेरी खुली जुल्फें बिखेर दे, बस यही दुआ करता है,

फिर अपनी उँगलियों से उन्हें प्यार से संवारता है।

उसका यूँ बेलौस बदतमीजियां करना मेरे रुखसार को याकूत कर देता है।

तेरा चेहरा बहुत नूरानी है वो हमेशा यही कहता है।

उसके यार दोस्त मुझे भाभी बुलाए तो उन्हें फटकारता है,

बुरा नहीं लगता उसे पर वो ऐसा जताता है।

असल में तो वो भी मुस्काता है, शर्माता है।

और किसी को इल्म नही है, ये बात सिर्फ मुझे पता है।

यूं तो बेखौफ भीड़ में मेरा हाथ पकड़ कर चलता है,

हमारे रिश्ते पर उसे ग़ुरूर है, वो हमेशा यही कहता है।

तमन्ना

कल रात की नींद मुझे वो ख्वाब दिखा गई,

जिसके मुकम्मल होने का ख्वाब,

मैंने अपने ख्वाबों में भी देखा था।

एक सुबह मैंने दर्पण के सामने खड़े होकर अपने माथे पर सिंदूर

लगाया और अपने बदन पर एक साड़ी लपेटी।

जब एक कदम आगे बढ़ाया तो एक झंकार की आवाज़ आयी,

नहीं, ये मेरी पायल नहीं थी।

ये तुम्हारे घर की चाबियों का वो छल्ला है,

जो तुम्हारी माँ ने मुझे सौंपा था।

और शायद मेरी कमर पर शोर करके, ये चाबियाँ एक बार फिर से

मुझे मेरी उन ज़िम्मेदारियों से रूबरू करवाना चाहती है,

जिन्हें मैं हमेशा से निभाना चाहती थी।

जब बाहर निकली तो तुम बिस्तर पर बैठे कुछ सोच रहे थे,

या शायद तुम मेरा ही इंतेज़ार कर रहे थे।

फिर मुझे देखकर, तुमने मेरे हाथ थमा, सजदा किया

और कहा, "आज मेरी बरसों की तमन्ना पूरी हो गयी,

मेरी सुबह में तुम जो शामिल हो गयी"।

इतवार

एक रोज़ मैं भी बैठी थी कुछ लिखने,

सोचा तेरे लिए कविता लिखूँ।

पर लफ़्ज़ों ने भी हार मान ली,

कहा कि हम बयां नही कर पाएंगे।

फिर ख़याल आया

हमारे किस्सों को कहानी का रूप दूं,

पर एक डर सता रहा था,

कहीं किसी ने मेरी डायरी पढ़ ली

तो सारे ज़माने को खबर हो जाएगी।

फिर कलम रखकर, पलकें झुकाकर,

तेरी कल्पना में खो गयी।

कैसे तू मेरा नजरबट्टू बना रहता था।

कैसे मुझे देख हौले से मुस्कुरा देता था,

फिर कैसे जवाब में मैं अपनी पलकें झुका दिया करती थी।

कैसे आऊँ अब होश में,

तू उस इतवार जैसा है जिसे मैं कभी खोना नही चाहती हूँ।

अलसायी सी, बेफिक्र सी, मैं तेरी बाहों में सोना चाहती हूँ।

Harsh Bhadoriya

He is Harsh Bhadoriya. He is presenting his talent of writing since the past two years. Writing wasn't his first choice but now it has become his forever thing. Now he takes away people from one world to other with his words. He has worked in many anthologies as a co-author. You can contact him via -- Email- bharsh714@gmail.com Instagram- @bharsh06

तुम वापस आओगी क्या?

मेरा दिल बेहाल हो गया है, उसको तुम संभालोगी क्या?

जैसे तुम मेरी फिकर किया करती थी उस तरह से अब करोगी क्या?

हाँ जनता हूं में की अब वक़्त बदल गया है।

मगर तुम इसे दोबारा बदलने आओगी क्या?

हो सके तो आना जरूर।

मेरा दिल जो बिखर गया है उसको आके संभाल ना जरूर।

पर क्या तुम मुझे फिर से उसी तरह मिलपाओगी क्या?

तुम वापस आओगी क्या?

याद आती है तुम्हारी इतनी की बता नहीं सकता।

जज्बातजो दबे हुए है उन्हें और दबा नहीं सकता।

हमने जो प्यार किया उसे फिर से जगाने आओगी क्या?

तुम वापस आओगी क्या?

कैंटीन में बैठकर जो मस्ती की वो याद है न?

चेट्स पे हमने जो बाते करी वो याद है न?

शायद में कुछ बातें भूल रहा हूं।

तुम मुझे याद करवाओगी क्या?

तुम वापस आओगी क्या?

माफ़ कर दो मुझे उस दिन के लिए जब तुमसे गुस्से में कहा था।

पर तुम ही तो समझती हो कि में क्या महसूस कर रहा था।

पर क्या तुम इस बार मुझे माफ कर पाओगी क्या?

बोलो न तुम वापस आओगी क्या?

<u>वो मेरी **** है।।</u>

एक लड़की है जो बहोत सच्ची है।

मुझे जिसकी हर बात लगती अच्छीहै।

जाने क्या बात है उस मे ऐसी।

उसे देखा तब से दिल में बसीहै।।

आंखे जिसकी बहोत प्यारी है।

दिल करे डूब जाने को।

एक बार जो देख ले उनको।

मुश्किल हो जाए नज़र हटाने को।।

मुस्कान में जिसकी एक जादू सा है।

देख कर दिल हो जाता बेकाबू सा है।

जिसकी हस्सी के लिए हर चीज़ कर सकता हूं।

जिसके बारे में सोचके में हर पल हस सकताहूं।।

जो पास हो तो लगे दुनिया मिल गई।

जो दूर जाए तो लगे हर चीज़ छीन गई।

छोड़ने के बारे में जिसको में सोच नहीं सकता।

जिसके बिना सवेरा मेरा अच्छा हो नहीं सकता।।

जिसके पास मेरे दिल की चाबीहै।

जिसके दिल में बचपना अभी बाहोत बाकीहै।

जिसकी हरकते मुझे करती खुशहै।

जो पास हो तो मुझे नहीं किसी बात का दुखहै।।

वक़्त बदलता तो शायद उसे भुला भी देते। पर ये तो बस गुजरता जा रहा है।।

में उनकी हर दुआ की गुज़ारिश बनने की कोशिश में लगा रहा पर उन्होंने इश्क़ किसी और का कुबूल कर लिया।।

उनके लिए मुझे भूलना तो आसा नही था और मैनें अपनी दुआओ में उनकी खुशी मांग के उसे और आसान कर दिया।।

तुम जा चुकी हो दूर मुझसे फिर भी तुम्हारा इंतजार करता हूं, हाथ में है मेरी ज़िन्दगी (कलम) फिर भी तुमसे प्यार करता हूं।।

Shivansh Sharma

He is Shivansh Sharma from Indore, currently in Mysore for Studying. He loves to write his thoughts in the form of poems, shayaris etc. He loves to make new friends. He always believes in true love with long term relationship rather than short term relationship.

दूरियां

कैसा है ये इश्क़ तेरा मेरा तेरे बिनलगता नहीं जिया मेरा,

तुझ से दूर जो होता हूं तन्हा-तन्हा रहता हूं,

जैसे गिर पड़े हो बादल मुझ पर औस दिल पर छा जाती है तेरे बिना

होली भी फीकी है,

तेरे बिन दिए है दीवाली,

तेरी एक झलक को हम बेसबर-ए-बेखबर,

तुझे देखकर जैसे चलती हो पवन।

पतंग और डोर

पतंग और डोर जैसा है इश्क़ तेरा मेरा,

जब पेच लड़ते तो सुलझना नहीं आया,

उड़ते रहे तेरे इश्क में बेकाबू,

समझ के हवा के विपरित था मनाना आया,

मांझा पकड़ा था प्यारी से उम्मीद से लूटते रहे तेरे प्यार में बचना नहीं

आया,

पेच तो लड़ गए प्यार में मगर सुलझाना नहीं आया।

अनजाना, अनजानी

थी अनजानी अनसुलझी सी शुरुवात थे

हम एक दूसरे से अनजान,

मुलाकात तो हुई थी कभी किसी गली- चोबारा पे थोड़ी सी

खट्टी मीठी सी तकरार,

सोचाना था दोस्त भी बनेंगे होगा थोड़ा इकरार,

पता नहीं क्या था उस फिजा में जो हम दम बन बैठे,

अब है एक दूसरे के लिए सम्मान और प्यार,

तेरा वो दूर हो कर प्यार के लिए लड़ना झगड़ना याद है

मुझे, तेरा वो पास होकर फिकर करना बहुत रास है मुझे,

तू यूहीं रहे हमेशा मेरे संग यहीं दुआ है खुदा से मेरे हम दम।।

तू ही

मेरी सोनी मेरी तमन्ना तू है इतनी हसी,

की तू ना हो तो ना बघो में है बाहर,

ना ही झरनों में हो झंकार ,

ना ही पत्तों की सरसराहट नहीं ,

ना ही झूमती हवाओं का दीदार ,

तू ही तो है सब कुछ है वरना कुछ भी नहीं कुछ भी नहीं...

तुम्हे खोजता ढूंढ़ता फिरता है

ये मन दर बदर और कहता रहता पल पल की तुम यहीं हो तुम यहीं हो

!

हर पल

मेरी ज़िन्दगी का हर पल तुझसे शुरू तुझपे ख़तम ,

मेरी लिखावट की शुरुवात तुझि से और तुझ पर ही अंत,

तू ही है ख्वाबों में ख़यालो मे,

तू ही है जज्बातों में इरादों में,

तू है तो सब है गुल-ए-बहार,

तू नहीं तो सब है वीरान,

तू ही तो सुबह भी शाम,

वरना रात भी है बंजर,

तू है तो सब कुछ है वरना कुछ भी नहीं..